PRIDE & PREJUDICE

Jane Austen

LEVEL 3

Adapted by: Jane Rollason
Fact Files written by: Jacquie Bloese
Publisher: Jacquie Bloese
Editor: Matthew Hancock
Designer: Dawn Wilson
Picture research: Emma Bree and Osha Mason

Photo credits:
Cover and interior photos: courtesy of Universal Studios
Licensing LLLP
Page 38: W. Bibikow/Alamy.
Page 48: P. Adams/Alamy.
Page 54: T. Graham/Corbis.
Pages 78 & 79: S. Honda/AFP/Getty Images; Pan
Macmillan/Picador; Headline/Review.
Pages 82 & 83: Mary Evans; Visual Arts Library/Alamy.

Mary Glasgow Magazines (Scholastic Ltd.)
Euston House
24 Eversholt Street
London NW1 IDB

Printed in Singapore

Contents

Page

◀ MR DARCY

Mr Darcy is a very rich and proud young man. He has a sister, Georgiana, who is ten years younger than him. He owns a large estate called Pemberley in Derbyshire.

THE BENNET FAMILY ▶

The Bennet family live at Longbourn. They are (from left to right) Lydia (the youngest daughter), Mr Bennet, Jane (the oldest daughter), Mrs Bennet, Kitty, Elizabeth and Mary.

MR BINGLEY ▶

Mr Bingley is a rich and charming young man. He comes to live at Netherfield Park near the Bennets in Hertfordshire. He and Mr Darcy are good friends.

MR COLLINS ▼

Mr Collins is a cousin of the Bennet family. He is a clergyman and his church is on the large estate of Lady Catherine de Bourgh.

MR WICKHAM ▲

Mr Wickham is a charming and handsome young man. He joins the officers in Meryton, near Longbourn, and is a favourite of the Bennet girls. Mr Darcy does not like him, though …

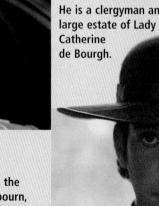

LADY CATHERINE DE BOURGH ▶

Lady Catherine de Bourgh is Mr Darcy's rich aunt. She has one daughter and they live at Rosings Park.

Newcastle

Pemberley

Netherfield Park
Meryton
Longbourn
London
Rosings Park
Brighton

◀ PLACES

Elizabeth's uncle and aunt, the Gardiners, live in London. The Bingleys and Mr Darcy usually spend the winter there.
Brighton is a town by the sea. The officers move here from Meryton during the story.

The language of Jane Austen's time

Pride and Prejudice *was written in 1813. The English that people spoke at that time was a little different from modern English. Here are some of the differences that you will find when you read* Pride and Prejudice.

Jane Austen's language	modern English
did not, are not, etc.	*didn't, aren't, etc.*
I wish to ...	*I want to ...*
to admire	*to like or to fancy*
a handsome woman	*a beautiful woman*
shall	*will*

People did not use first names, except with their families. So Mr Darcy calls Elizabeth Miss Elizabeth *or* Miss Elizabeth Bennet. *Even husbands and wives often called each other as* Mrs Bennet *and* Mr Bennet!

PRIDE & PREJUDICE
CHAPTER 1
The Meryton ball

'Mr Bennet, have you heard the news?' Mrs Bennet said one day. 'A young man with a large fortune is coming to live at Netherfield Park!'

'What is his name and is he married or single?' asked Mr Bennet.

'His name is Bingley and he is single, my dear! What a fine thing for our girls!'

'Why is that, my dear?'

'Oh, Mr Bennet, you are so difficult! Of course he must marry one of them. You must go and visit him as soon as he arrives.'

'I will tell him he may marry any of our five daughters, but I will suggest Lizzy.'

'You will not! Lizzy is no better than the others. She is not as pretty as Jane and not as much fun as Lydia,' replied Mrs Bennet crossly. Elizabeth was quick and clever, but Mrs Bennet was not, and she admired Jane and Lydia more.

* * *

Mr Bennet was one of the first of Mr Bingley's new neighbours to visit him. But Mr Bennet loved to laugh at his wife and did not tell her until after his visit.

That evening, the family were in the sitting room. Lizzy was putting some flowers on a hat.

'I hope Mr Bingley will like your hat, Lizzy,' said Mr Bennet.

'How do we know what Mr Bingley will like?' cried Mrs Bennet. 'We are not going to visit him.'

'When is the next ball, Lizzy?' continued Mr Bennet.

'In a fortnight, in Meryton,' said Elizabeth.

'Yes,' said Mrs Bennet crossly, 'and our girls will not be able to dance with Mr Bingley because *you* have not visited him! Oh, I am sick of hearing about Mr Bingley.'

'I am sorry to hear that, my dear,' said Mr Bennet. 'Because I wanted to tell you about my visit to him this morning.'

The effect was just as Mr Bennet had hoped. The ladies all called out questions at once.

'Oh girls, what an excellent father you have!' said Mrs Bennet, when she was calmer.

✳✳✳

The Meryton ball had already started when Mr Bingley arrived with his two sisters and another young man.

Mr Bingley was good-looking and had perfect manners. His friend Mr Darcy was tall and handsome. News quickly went round the ballroom that Mr Darcy had a large fortune and everyone admired him at once. They soon discovered that he was proud, however, and then he was not so popular.

Mr Bingley danced every dance and was charming. He was very friendly to Jane, the oldest of the Bennet girls, and danced with her twice. Mr Darcy danced once with each of Bingley's sisters and refused to speak to any other lady in the room. Nobody liked him and they all hoped he would never come again. Mrs Bennet disliked him most of all, because he did not dance with any of her daughters.

Elizabeth did not join two of the dances because there were not enough gentlemen. She heard some of the conversation between Mr Bingley and Mr Darcy.

'Come, Darcy, you must dance. Do not stand by yourself.'

'I shall not dance. I hate dancing. I have danced with your sisters and I will not dance with any other woman in the room.'

'I have never met so many nice girls in my life. Some of them are very pretty.'

'You are dancing with the only pretty girl here,' said Mr Darcy, looking at Jane.

'She is the most beautiful girl I ever saw,' said Mr Bingley. 'But one of her sisters is very pretty too. She is sitting just behind us.'

Mr Darcy looked round at Elizabeth. 'She is not pretty enough to interest me,' he said coldly. 'Return to your partner and enjoy her smiles. Do not worry about me.'

✳✳✳

Later that evening, Jane told Elizabeth that she liked Mr Bingley very much.

'I was very surprised when he asked me for a second dance,' she said.

'Were you?' replied Elizabeth. 'Nobody else in the room was surprised. You were five times prettier than any other woman there. Well, he is very charming and I will allow you to like him. What about his sisters, though? They are certainly very fine and good-looking, but their manners are not so good. Meryton did not seem good enough for them.'

'Caroline Bingley was very nice to me,' replied Jane. 'She is coming to live at Netherfield with her brother.'

'Dear Jane, you never see a fault in anybody,' Elizabeth smiled.

CHAPTER 2
Dinners and dances

The Bennets and the Bingleys met several times over the next fortnight, at dinners given by their neighbours. Mr Bingley clearly admired Jane. Elizabeth knew that Jane also admired Mr Bingley. The rest of the world did not know, however, because Jane hid her feelings. She was always kind and charming to everyone.

Elizabeth discussed this with her friend Charlotte Lucas.

'If she hides her feelings too well,' said Charlotte, 'Bingley may lose interest. They do not see each other often. Jane should make the most of every half hour she has with him. When they are engaged, she will have plenty of time to fall in love.'

'Your plan would be good,' said Elizabeth, 'if you only wanted to get a rich husband. But that is not Jane's way. She has only known him a fortnight.'

'A fortnight is as good as a year when you are choosing a husband. Happiness in marriage happens by chance. The less you know about them, the better.'

'You make me laugh, Charlotte! You know you would never act this way.'

＊＊＊

Elizabeth watched Jane and Bingley. She did not realise that someone was also watching her. Mr Darcy had not admired Elizabeth at the Meryton ball, but he now began to change his mind. Her beautiful dark eyes made her face look very intelligent. He liked her warm character and her natural manners. Elizabeth had no idea of his feelings. She only knew that she was not pretty enough for him to dance with.

After dinner, the younger Lucas and Bennet girls started some dancing. Mr Bingley and Jane joined them.

Sir William Lucas, Charlotte's father, came and spoke to Mr Darcy.

'How charming this is!' he said. 'Do you dance often, sir?'

'As little as possible,' answered Mr Darcy.

Sir William Lucas smiled. Elizabeth was near them and he called to her. 'Miss Elizabeth, why are you not dancing? Mr Darcy, you cannot refuse to dance with such a beautiful lady!'

But before he could answer, Elizabeth stepped back.

'I do not wish to dance, sir. Please do not think I was looking for a partner.'

Mr Darcy asked Elizabeth very politely to dance. But again Elizabeth refused and turned away.

As Mr Darcy watched her go, Miss Caroline Bingley came to his side.

'I can guess your thoughts,' she said to him. 'You are thinking how awful these evenings in the country are. So many people, yet so little interesting conversation.'

'You are wrong. I was thinking that a pair of fine eyes in the face of a pretty woman is a very lovely thing.'

'And which young lady has put these thoughts in your head?' asked Caroline.

'Miss Elizabeth Bennet.'

'I am amazed,' said Caroline. 'How long has she been a favourite? And when is the wedding day?'

'Your imagination moves too quickly,' said Mr Darcy. 'For you, admiration becomes love and love becomes marriage in a second.'

CHAPTER 3
At Netherfield

Mr Bennet was not a very rich man. His Longbourn estate earned only two thousand pounds a year. And unhappily for his daughters, they would not even get that when he died. Because he had no sons, his estate would go to a cousin called Mr Collins.

This fact upset Mrs Bennet greatly when she thought of it. Mrs Bennet had a little money of her own. When her father died, he had left her four thousand pounds. She had a sister in Meryton, Mrs Philips, and a rich brother in London with a successful business.

∗∗∗

Longbourn was half an hour's walk from the little town of Meryton. The younger Bennet girls, Kitty and Lydia, walked there three or four times a week to visit their aunt and the hat shop. And now Meryton had a new attraction. Some officers in red coats had just arrived in Meryton and were staying for the whole winter. Kitty, Lydia and Mrs Bennet could imagine no greater happiness.

∗∗∗

The family were sitting at lunch. Kitty and Lydia talked of nothing but officers.

'Well, my dear girls,' said Mr Bennet, when there was quiet, 'you must be two of the silliest girls in the country.'

Lydia paid her father no attention. 'I like Captain Carter,' she said. 'I must see him this afternoon as he is going to London tomorrow.'

'How can you call your own children silly?' asked Mrs Bennet. 'I remember a time when I liked a red coat … and if a young officer with five or six thousand a year would like one of my girls, I will not say no to him.'

At that moment a servant came in with a note from Netherfield for Jane.

'Well, Jane, what does it say?' asked Mrs Bennet.

'It is from Caroline Bingley,' said Jane. 'It is an invitation to dinner today. Can I have the carriage?'

'No, Jane, you must go on horseback. I think it will rain. And then you will have to stay the night.'

✳✳✳

A few minutes after Jane had left, it began to rain hard. The rain continued all evening and Jane did not return. The next morning, a note came for Elizabeth.

'My dearest Lizzy,' she read, 'I got very wet yesterday and feel unwell this morning. My kind friends say I cannot return home until I am better. They have called Dr Jones.'

'Well, my dear,' said Mr Bennet to his wife. 'If your daughter dies, we can be happy that it was for a good reason.'

'Oh!' said Mrs Bennet. 'People do not die of colds. The Bingleys will take care of her.'

But Elizabeth was worried. She could not have the carriage, so she decided to walk the three miles to Netherfield.

***

The servant at Netherfield took Elizabeth into the breakfast room. Mr Bingley's sisters were coldly polite, though Mr Bingley was kind and welcoming. Elizabeth went at once to Jane, who was upstairs in bed.

'I cannot believe it,' laughed Caroline Bingley after she had left the room. 'She has walked three miles in this horrible weather. Did you see how dirty her skirts are?'

'I did not notice her skirts,' said Mr Darcy. 'But the exercise certainly made her eyes brighter.'

***

Jane was really unwell, and Elizabeth was glad she had come. The doctor said she must not leave her bed. Elizabeth was invited to stay at Netherfield until Jane was better. Her clothes were sent from Longbourn.

***

Elizabeth spent the day with Jane and joined everyone downstairs for dinner. Mr Bingley was charming, but the others did not speak to her much. Caroline Bingley spoke only to Mr Darcy. Elizabeth returned to Jane as soon as the meal was finished. Caroline at once told the room that Miss Elizabeth Bennet had no style, no conversation, no manners and was not beautiful.

'Jane is such a sweet girl,' said Louisa, Mr Bingley's other sister. 'I hope she will find a good husband. But with her mother and father and her awful younger sisters, I'm afraid there is no chance of it!'

When Jane finally fell asleep, Elizabeth came downstairs. Everyone was playing cards, so she found a book to read.

'I love to read,' said Caroline, laying down the six of

hearts. 'You have such a good library at Pemberley, Mr Darcy. You are always buying books.'

'We have built up our library over many years,' replied Mr Darcy. 'I plan to continue the work.'

'And how is your sister, Mr Darcy? Is she as tall as me yet?'

'I think she is the same height as Miss Elizabeth Bennet,' replied Mr Darcy.

'She is so pretty and has such good manners. And she plays the piano beautifully.'

'I am always amazed that young ladies can do so many things!' said Mr Bingley.

'I cannot agree,' said Mr Darcy. 'I do not know more than six young ladies who are really clever.'

'Oh yes,' said Caroline Bingley. 'A woman must know music, singing, dancing, drawing and modern languages. And she must walk and speak charmingly.'

'In that case,' said Elizabeth to Mr Darcy, 'I am surprised you know any such women.'

***

The next day passed in the same way. In the evening, however, the card table did not appear. Mr Darcy asked the ladies for some music. The two Bingley sisters moved quickly to the piano. While they were playing and singing, Elizabeth noticed that Mr Darcy often looked at her. 'He is deciding what is wrong with me,' she thought. Well, she did not like him and did not care what he thought of her.

'Does the music make you want to dance, Miss Bennet?' asked Mr Darcy.

'I do not know how to answer, Mr Darcy. If I say "Yes", then you will think I have bad taste. So I will say "No", Mr Darcy, I would not like to dance. Now you may not think badly of me.'

'I certainly do not think badly of you.'

Elizabeth was surprised. In fact, Mr Darcy thought well of her. Her answers were both sweet and clever. He was in danger of falling in love with her. Only her terrible family stopped him.

Caroline Bingley was beginning to notice Darcy's interest in Elizabeth. She hoped her friend Jane would get better soon. That evening, Jane was well enough to come downstairs after dinner. Everyone welcomed her. Mr Bingley piled wood on the fire and moved Jane nearer to it. Then he sat next to her and talked to her all evening. Mr Darcy began to read. Caroline did the same, but she soon became tired of it.

'Charles,' she called to her brother, 'are you really going to have a ball at Netherfield? You may find we do not all enjoy it.'

'If you mean Darcy,' replied her brother, 'he may go to bed before it begins. I plan to send out invitations next week.'

Miss Bingley got up and began to walk around the room. She looked very fine, but Mr Darcy did not notice. He continued to read his book. She tried again to get his attention.

'Miss Elizabeth Bennet,' she said. 'Please join me for a walk around the room.'

Mr Darcy looked up. Caroline invited him to join them too, but he refused.

'You can only have two reasons for walking around the room,' said Mr Darcy.

'What can you mean?' asked Caroline.

'You either have secret things to discuss. Or you want me to admire you as you walk. In the first case, I would be in the way. In the second case, I can admire you much better if I sit by the fire.'

'Mr Darcy! How can we allow him such a speech!' cried Miss Bingley.

'We must laugh at him,' replied Elizabeth.

'I am afraid we cannot laugh at him. He is too serious and intelligent.'

'Does Mr Darcy have a perfect character?' Elizabeth asked Miss Bingley.

'No,' said Darcy. 'I have faults. I cannot easily forget other people's offences. When someone has lost my good opinion, it is lost forever.'

'That is a fault! But I cannot laugh at it. You are safe from me,' said Elizabeth.

∗∗∗

The next day, Elizabeth and Jane finally returned to Longbourn. Mrs Bennet was not pleased to see them; she felt sure Jane was not well enough to leave Netherfield. She was afraid Mr Bingley needed more time to fall in love with her daughter. Their father, however, had missed them. Evening conversation at Longbourn was boring and silly without them.

CHAPTER 4
Mr Collins

'I hope you have planned a good dinner today,' said Mr Bennet to his wife the next morning. 'We are expecting a guest. He is a gentleman and a stranger.'

'Who do you mean, my dear?' asked Mrs Bennet. 'I hope all my dinners are good enough for anyone!'

'It is my cousin, Mr Collins. He is now a clergyman in a place called Hunsford. And as soon as I am dead, he may throw you all out of this house.'

'Oh, my dear!' cried Mrs Bennet. 'Do not speak of that horrible man.'

'He is arriving at four o'clock this afternoon and staying until next Saturday.'

✷✷✷

Mr Collins was at the front door at four o'clock. He was a serious young man with very polite manners.

'You have a fine family of beautiful daughters, Mrs Bennet,' he said, 'and I am sure they will all soon be married.'

'You are very kind, sir. I hope you are right. If not, they will have nothing.'

'You are perhaps thinking of the future of the Longbourn estate.'

'I am, sir. It is a terrible

business for my poor girls. I know it is not your fault. Everything in this world is chance.'

Mr Collins admired everything in the house – the dining room, the hall, the furniture. They went in to dinner and he admired the meal too.

After dinner, Mr Collins told the family about Lady Catherine de Bourgh. Lady Catherine had given Mr Collins his position as a clergyman only two months before. The church was on the edge of her very large estate, called Rosings Park. She took a great interest in the lives of everyone around her. Mr Collins could not stop talking of Lady Catherine. He became even more serious and his eyes shone as he talked of her character and her importance in the world. When Lady Catherine came to the church on Sunday, she had listened to Mr Collins with approval. She had already invited him to dinner twice at Rosings Park. Once she visited his small home. She approved of the changes he was making. In fact, she was even kind enough to suggest putting some cupboards in a bedroom.

'She has also suggested that I marry as soon as I can,' said Mr Collins, 'as long as I choose carefully.'

'Well, well, Mr Collins,' said Mr Bennet, when he stopped speaking for a moment. 'It is a pity that great ladies in general are not more like her. Her husband, I believe, is dead. Does she have any family?'

'She has one charming daughter. As Lady Catherine says, you can see Miss de Bourgh's high class in her face. And that is more important than being pretty. Unhappily, she is rather weak and often ill. She would play the piano brilliantly, if she were able to take lessons. She is kind enough to drive by my small home often in her carriage.'

'Is she often in London?' asked Mrs Bennet.

'Sadly her health does not allow her to go to town. As I told Lady Catherine one day, London has never seen its brightest star. Lady Catherine seemed pleased with the idea. I am happy to say these little things – I know the ladies like them.'

'You are lucky to be able to think of such things to say, Mr Collins,' said Mr Bennet. 'Tell me, do you think of them at the time of speaking or do you prepare them before?'

'Generally the conversation at the time suggests them to me. Sometimes I prepare a few things to say in quiet moments, but I like them to sound natural.'

Mr Bennet greatly enjoyed listening to Mr Collins. He liked his high opinion of his own importance and his silly character.

✳✳✳

Mr Collins was ready to marry. He had his church, his small home and Lady Catherine. All he needed was a wife, and his plan was to choose one of the Bennet daughters. One day he would get the Longbourn estate. It was only fair that he should marry one of them.

For the first evening, Jane was his choice. During a short conversation with Mrs Bennet the following morning, however, he learned that he was too late. Mrs Bennet expected another gentleman to propose to Jane very soon. While Mrs Bennet was pouring a second cup of tea, his attention moved from Jane to Elizabeth.

CHAPTER 5
Mr Wickham

Mr Collins joined the Bennet girls on a walk to Meryton. They entered the town, and Lydia, the youngest daughter, at once saw Mr Denny, her favourite officer. He was walking along the main street with a very handsome gentleman. This young man had already caught the attention of every young lady in the town. Lydia and Kitty made their way to the hat shop, which Mr Denny was just passing.

'May I introduce my friend, Mr Wickham?' said Mr Denny to Lydia and Kitty. 'Mr Wickham is joining the officers here in Meryton.'

Mr Wickham was tall and charming. Just then, Darcy and Bingley rode up on horseback. They were on their way to Longbourn to find out if Jane was better. Darcy smiled, but suddenly noticed Mr Wickham. His smile disappeared. Elizabeth was amazed at the effect of the meeting on the two men. Both were shocked. What could it mean? Mr Darcy turned his horse and rode away. Bingley followed soon after.

∗∗∗

The next evening, Aunt Philips invited the Bennets, Mr Collins and some of the officers to dinner. Mr Wickham chose to sit next to Elizabeth. He soon introduced the subject she most wanted to talk about – how he knew Mr Darcy.

'How long has Mr Darcy been at Netherfield?' he asked.

'About a month,' she said. 'He has a large estate in Derbyshire, I understand.'

'Yes,' replied Wickham. 'I believe it brings in ten

thousand pounds a year. No one can tell you more about it than me – I have known him since we were children.'

Elizabeth was surprised.

'Perhaps you saw the look that passed between us yesterday? It was a very cold meeting, was it not? Do you know Mr Darcy well?'

'As well as I want to!' cried Elizabeth. 'I have spent four days in the same house as him, and I do not like him. He is not popular in Hertfordshire. Everyone dislikes his pride.'

'Is he staying at Netherfield much longer?' asked Wickham.

'I do not know,' said Elizabeth, 'but I hope you will not change your plans to be in Meryton because of it.'

'Certainly not! I will not be the one to leave. If *I* offend *him*, *he* must go. He has acted badly towards me. His father was one of the best men in the world. He was my truest friend and I have missed him greatly since he died some years ago. I was trained for the church and I would now have my own church, except for Mr Darcy.'

'Really?'

'Yes. Mr Darcy's father promised me a lovely church in Derbyshire. But when the old clergyman left two years ago, Mr Darcy gave it to another man.'

'Why?' cried Elizabeth.

'He said I spent money too freely. I was too wild. I get angry easily and perhaps I have sometimes given my opinion of Mr Darcy too honestly. But the fact is, we are different sorts of men, and he hates me.'

'I am quite shocked,' said Elizabeth. 'Do others know about this?'

'No, I will never tell the world. I loved his father too well to speak badly of his son.'

Elizabeth approved of these feelings and thought he looked more handsome than ever.

'And how do you explain his actions?'

'He has never liked me. We were both born at Pemberley; we lived there together. My father managed his father's estate. Mr Darcy thought his father loved me too much.'

'Although I did not like Mr Darcy before, I did not think he was as bad as this,' said Elizabeth. 'Has his pride ever done any good?'

'His family pride makes him generous to the poor. His brotherly pride makes him kind to his sister.'

'What sort of a girl is Miss Darcy?'

'She was a sweet child and liked me very much. But she is nothing to me now. She is handsome, about fifteen, and very clever, I hear. I also hear that she has her brother's pride. Since her father's death, she has lived in London, I believe.'

***

Mr Collins, meanwhile, was losing every point at the card table. Wickham heard Mr Collins talking about Lady Catherine de Bourgh to Mrs Philips. He asked Elizabeth if Mr Collins knew Lady Catherine, and Elizabeth explained his situation.

'You know of course that Lady Catherine and Mr Darcy's mother were sisters?' said Wickham. 'She is Mr Darcy's aunt. Lady Catherine's daughter will have a very large fortune one day. The idea has always been for the two cousins to marry and join the two estates of Rosings Park and Pemberley.'

This information made Elizabeth smile. Poor Caroline Bingley! There was no hope for her, then!

At Longbourn the next morning, Elizabeth told Jane Wickham's story. Jane was at first shocked and then refused to believe it. The whole thing was clearly a mistake.

'Dear Lizzy,' said Jane, 'is it not possible that everyone is wrong about Mr Darcy's character? Mr Bingley would not be friends with such a man.'

'But why would Mr Wickham make up a story like this? I could check the facts so easily.'

'I do not know what to think,' answered Jane.

'Jane, you can never think badly of anyone,' said Elizabeth. 'But I am sorry, I know exactly what to think!'

At that moment, Mr Bingley and his sisters arrived at Longbourn. They came with an invitation to the Netherfield ball. The two sisters were very pleased to see Jane. They avoided Mrs Bennet as much as possible, said very little to Elizabeth and nothing to the others. They did not stay long. In fact, they seemed in a terrible hurry to leave.

Although Elizabeth avoided speaking to Mr Collins as much as possible, she asked him if he was going to the ball. Yes, he explained, as it was a ball given by a young man of good character. Both the church and Lady Catherine would approve, he felt sure.

'And I would like to ask you, my dear cousin, for the first two dances!'

'Of course, thank you,' said Elizabeth. Oh well! She would just have to wait before dancing with Wickham. She began to realise, however, that Mr Collins was now thinking of *her* as the future Mrs Collins. It was not long before she also realised that her mother approved of the idea. Elizabeth pretended not to notice and hoped that Mr Collins would never make the offer.

CHAPTER 6
The Netherfield ball

The Netherfield ball did not start well for Elizabeth. When she entered the ballroom, she learned from Mr Denny that Mr Wickham had gone to London on business the day before.

'Perhaps he wished to avoid a certain gentleman!' smiled Mr Denny.

So it was Mr Darcy's fault. She did not now expect to enjoy the ball.

The two first dances made her more unhappy. Mr Collins danced badly and Elizabeth was deeply embarrassed.

Elizabeth had a naturally happy character, however.

Soon she was in lively conversation with her friend, Charlotte Lucas and laughing at her cousin, Mr Collins.

Suddenly, Mr Darcy was at her side. He asked her for the next dance, and before she could think of a reason to say 'No,' she said 'Yes'.

Their conversation during the dance was polite but cold. Why had Mr Darcy asked her? He did not seem to enjoy it. And then they came to the subject she really wanted to discuss.

'Do you and your sisters often walk to Meryton?' Mr Darcy asked.

'Yes. When we saw you the other day, we were just meeting someone new.'

The effect on Mr Darcy was immediate. He became even colder and said, 'Mr Wickham is always able to *make* friends. He is not always able to *keep* them.'

'He has been unlucky to lose you as a friend.'

At that moment, Sir William Lucas came between them

and the conversation ended.

'I hope we shall see more of this wonderful dancing, Mr Darcy, after a certain wedding takes place.' Here Sir William smiled at Elizabeth, before looking towards Jane and Mr Bingley. Mr Darcy was surprised by these words and for a moment looked very seriously at his friend and Jane.

✳✳✳

Later that evening, Elizabeth found Jane and asked what she had learned of Mr Wickham.

'Mr Bingley does not know Mr Wickham or his history. But he is sure that Mr Darcy has been kinder to Mr Wickham than was necessary. Mr Wickham has spent too freely and has lost Mr Darcy's good opinion through his own fault.'

'This will not change my opinion,' Elizabeth replied. 'Mr Bingley gets his story from Mr Darcy.'

At supper, Elizabeth was not pleased to find herself very near her mother. Even worse, her mother was next to Lady Lucas. This gave Mrs Bennet the chance to discuss Jane and Mr Bingley. She had enough to say on the subject to last for the whole dinner. Although Mrs Bennet whispered, Elizabeth could see that Mr Darcy heard every word.

'Please, mother,' said Elizabeth. 'Speak more quietly. Why do you wish to offend Mr Darcy?'

'What is Mr Darcy to me?' replied her mother, loudly. 'Why should I be afraid of him?'

But there was more embarrassment to come for poor Elizabeth. Someone asked for some singing after dinner, and Mary Bennet came to the piano first. Mary sang one song very badly. After polite thanks from a nearby table, she began another. Mr Bennet jumped up to stop Mary singing a third. Mr Collins followed this with a long, boring talk about clergymen and singing. Many people in the room laughed – but *at* him and not *with* him. The two youngest Bennet girls, Lydia and Kitty, then ran through the room with some red-coated officers. They laughed and shouted like young children. Mr Darcy sat silently through all this. Elizabeth had never felt so ashamed and had never enjoyed a ball less.

Mrs Bennet, however, left the ball with a happy heart. She would soon have one daughter married to Mr Bingley and another to Mr Collins. And poor Lady Lucas had no married daughters at all. What could be better!

CHAPTER 7
An engagement

'Mrs Bennet,' said Mr Collins the next morning. 'May I speak privately with your lovely daughter Elizabeth?'

'Yes, of course, Mr Collins,' said Mrs Bennet. 'I shall go upstairs.'

'Mother, do not go,' said Elizabeth. 'Mr Collins can have nothing private to say to me. Please excuse me. I am going upstairs, too.'

'No, Lizzy. Stay where you are!' replied Mrs Bennet. And she gave her daughter a very cross look.

When Mr Collins and Elizabeth were alone, he spoke at once. He listed all the reasons for a clergyman to marry, Lady Catherine's views on the subject and his feelings of fairness towards Mr Bennet. Finally, he remembered his very strong feelings for Elizabeth. His proposal went on for so long that Elizabeth had to stop him.

'You forget, sir, that I have not given you an answer. Thank you for your proposal, but I must refuse.'

'I know very well,' replied Mr Collins with a smile, 'that young ladies refuse proposals two or even three times before they accept.'

'Mr Collins, I am not such a young lady! I am perfectly serious. You could not make me happy, and I am sure that I could not make you happy.'

Three more refusals were given but none was accepted. Elizabeth had to leave the room. When Mrs Bennet learned Elizabeth's answer from Mr Collins, she ran at once to Mr Bennet.

'Mr Bennet! You must make Lizzy marry Mr Collins. She says she will not have him!'

Elizabeth was called into the garden.

'Your mother says you must accept Mr Collins's proposal, my child,' said Mr Bennet.

'Yes, or I will never see her again,' said Mrs Bennet.

'An unhappy choice is before you,' her father continued. 'From this day you must be a stranger to one of your parents. Your mother will never see you again if you do *not* marry Mr Collins. I will never see you again if you *do*.'

Although Mr Collins's pride was hurt, his heart was hardly broken. Then Charlotte Lucas invited him to Lucas Lodge for the day, to make things easier for Elizabeth. He was happy to go.

Later that day, a letter arrived for Jane from Netherfield. It was from Caroline Bingley and it had some shocking news. The Bingleys and Mr Darcy had already left Netherfield and had no plans to return. Jane read part of the letter to Elizabeth:

I will not miss anything in Hertfordshire, except you, my dear friend. We will hope to see you again at some time in the future. And we must write often.

'Miss Bingley may not want her brother to be at Netherfield. That does not mean Mr Bingley will not come,' said Elizabeth.

'Let me read the part which hurts me,' said Jane.

Mr Darcy wishes to see his sister. And we wish to see her too. She is beautiful and clever. My brother admires her greatly – have I told you this before? – and he will now be able to see her very often. Louisa and I love her very much, and hope soon to have her as a sister.

'This is clear enough, Lizzy. Caroline does not expect *me* to be her sister. She has an idea of my feelings for her brother, and she is most kindly telling me that he has no interest in me.'

'Let me give you my opinion,' said Elizabeth. 'Miss Bingley sees that her brother is in love with you, and wants him to marry Miss Darcy. She hopes to keep him in town, and she wants you to think that he does not care about you.'

Jane shook her head.

'You must believe me!' said Elizabeth. 'She wants Miss Darcy for her brother, and she wants Mr Darcy for herself. We are not rich enough for them.'

'I do not share your opinion of Caroline,' Jane cried. 'She would not lie to me. How could I marry Mr Bingley, if I thought his sisters did not approve?'

'If their approval is more important than your happiness, then you must refuse him!'

Jane smiled. 'You know I would never do that!'

***

The last day of Mr Collins's visit to Longbourn arrived. Mrs Bennet said she hoped that he would visit them again soon. To everyone's amazement, he said he would come again as soon as Lady Catherine would allow. Mrs Bennet was sure he planned to propose to one of her younger daughters, perhaps Mary.

But the following morning, her hopes were destroyed.

Charlotte Lucas called after breakfast. She told Elizabeth privately that Mr Collins had proposed to her and she had accepted. They were engaged.

'Engaged to Mr Collins? My dear Charlotte – impossible!'

'Why are you so surprised, Elizabeth?' said Charlotte. She knew well that Mr Collins was neither sensible nor good company. 'I am not romantic, you know. I am twenty-seven and not pretty. I ask only for a comfortable home. I have as much chance of happiness with Mr Collins as most people on their wedding day.'

Elizabeth remembered her manners and wished Charlotte well. But she could not approve of Charlotte's explanation.

Sir William Lucas came to Longbourn the next day with news of his daughter's engagement to Mr Collins. Mrs Bennet was shocked and was not polite to Sir William. But he accepted the good wishes of Jane and Elizabeth happily. As soon as he had left, Mrs Bennet's feelings poured out. She did not believe it and she was sure they would never be happy.

Elizabeth was the main reason for all the trouble and a week passed before Mrs Bennet could speak to her daughter again.

'How nice it will be to have a daughter married!' Lady Lucas said to Mrs Bennet, more often than was necessary.

CHAPTER 8
Christmas at Longbourn

A second letter from Caroline Bingley made it clear that Netherfield would stay closed for the winter. Her brother Charles was staying with Mr Darcy in his London house, and the main subject of the letter was again Miss Darcy. Jane now believed that Mr Bingley had never had any special feelings for her. Elizabeth, however, was angry with Bingley. She was sure he loved her sister. Why did he let his sisters and Mr Darcy decide his future? And why did he not care about Jane's feelings?

Mr Wickham was very welcome at Longbourn. He was a bright light in dark days. His history with Mr Darcy was now generally known. Except for Jane Bennet, everybody in Hertfordshire thought Mr Darcy was the worst of men.

✷✷✷

Mrs Bennet's brother Mr Gardiner and his wife arrived for Christmas. Mr Gardiner was a sensible gentleman, cleverer and with better manners than his sister. Mrs Gardiner was handsome and intelligent, and a great favourite with Jane and Elizabeth.

As soon as Mrs Gardiner arrived, she gave out presents and described the latest fashions. It was then her turn to listen, and Mrs Bennet had much to tell her.

Later, Mrs Gardiner and Elizabeth walked together in the garden. Mrs Gardiner's first questions were about Jane. She knew about Mr Bingley from their letters.

'I am sorry nothing came of Mr Bingley's interest in Jane. But these things happen so often. A young man so easily falls in love with a pretty girl for a few weeks. And then he forgets her.'

'But he has not forgotten her. His friends have taken him away from her!'

'But was he *really* in love with her?'

'He didn't speak to anyone else in the room when Jane was there. At his own ball, he offended two or three young ladies when he didn't ask them to dance. I spoke to him twice myself, and he didn't answer me.'

'Poor Jane!' said Mrs Gardiner. 'That is real love. I am sorry for her, because she will not get over it quickly. You, Lizzy, would laugh about it and soon feel better. She feels things very deeply.'

During their stay, the Gardiners met Mr Wickham. Mrs Gardiner had once lived near Pemberley in Derbyshire, and she and Mr Wickham had much to talk about. She knew Mr Darcy's father, but nothing of the young Mr Darcy. She watched Elizabeth and Wickham together and could see there were feelings between them. However, she did not think Wickham was the right husband for Elizabeth.

'He has no money, Lizzy. I have nothing to say against him; he is an interesting young man. But you are clever and I am sure you will do what is right.'

'I am not in love with Mr Wickham, dear aunt. And I will not let him be in love with me.'

∗∗∗

Jane was deeply unhappy. Mrs Gardiner was worried about her and invited her to London. Jane was very pleased with the idea. She hoped to see her friend Caroline Bingley there, although she did not expect to see Mr Bingley.

Soon after the Gardiners and Jane left for London, Mr Collins returned to Hertfordshire. The day before her wedding, Charlotte came to see Elizabeth.

'Please write often,' said Charlotte. 'And will you come and see me?'

Elizabeth could not refuse, although she did not look forward to the visit.

'My father and sister are coming in March to Hunsford. I hope you will come too.'

***

A letter came from Jane in London. Jane had not had a reply to her letter from Caroline Bingley, so she had visited her house in Grosvenor Street. Jane wrote:

I did not think Caroline was feeling well, but she was glad to see me. She was cross because I had not told her I was coming to London. So, I was right. My last letter never reached her. Mr Bingley is busy with Mr Darcy, though they hardly ever see him. Miss Darcy was coming to dinner that evening. My visit was not long, as Caroline and her sister were going out.

Elizabeth shook her head. 'Bingley will not find out from his sister that Jane is in town,' she thought.

February passed and Jane saw nothing of Bingley or his sister. Finally Caroline Bingley visited Jane at the Gardiners, and Jane could no longer hide from the truth. Another letter arrived for Elizabeth.

My dearest Lizzy, you were right. Caroline has no feelings for me. She visited yesterday, and stayed a very short time. She did not say she wanted to see me again. I know that she wishes to protect her brother. But she need not worry. If he cared about me, we would have met by now. He knows I am in London, I am sure, from something she said. Write soon. I am looking forward to hearing about Hunsford when you are there.

✷✷✷

Mrs Gardiner did not need to worry about Mr Wickham. Elizabeth wrote to tell her that he now admired a young lady called Miss King. Miss King had one great attraction that Elizabeth did not have – a fortune of ten thousand pounds. Elizabeth accepted that he could not marry someone with no money. She did not approve of her friend Charlotte Lucas's reasons for marrying Mr Collins; but she was not so hard on Mr Wickham.

CHAPTER 9
Lady Catherine de Bourgh

Mr and Mrs Collins appeared at the door of their small Hunsford home. Sir William, his daughter Maria and Elizabeth got out of the carriage. Charlotte was very happy to see her friend, and Elizabeth was pleased she had come.

Mr Collins showed the visitors every point of interest of his small home – the furniture, the size of the rooms, the garden, the number of trees in each view. The best view of all was of Rosings Park, the home of Lady Catherine. It was a handsome modern building on a hill.

'Miss Elizabeth,' said Mr Collins, 'we are invited to dinner at Rosings! I am sure you will be very pleased with Lady Catherine. She is charming to my dear Charlotte. We go to dinner twice a week, and we are never allowed to walk home. She always orders her carriage for us.'

Mr Collins had advice for Elizabeth when it was time to get ready.

'Just wear your best clothes,' he said. 'Lady Catherine will like it if you are simply dressed. She likes people to dress correctly for their position in the world.'

Lady Catherine was large and tall, and perhaps she was once beautiful. Elizabeth saw something of Mr Darcy in her face. She was proud and cold, and when she spoke, she did not expect anyone to disagree with her. Miss de Bourgh, however, was thin and pale. She was not pretty and she spoke very little.

Mr Collins admired every dish that was brought to the table. Sir William repeated everything Mr Collins said.

After dinner, Lady Catherine talked until the coffee came. She gave advice to Charlotte about managing her home, her garden and her animals. Then she turned to Elizabeth and asked her many questions about her sisters, her family, her home and her father's carriage. Elizabeth answered all her questions politely, though she thought they were rude.

'Are any of your younger sisters out?*' she asked.

'Yes, all of them,' replied Elizabeth.

'What? All five out at once! How strange! The younger ones out before the older ones are married.'

'Should younger sisters have to wait for their older sisters to marry? I think that would be very hard. They have a right to enjoy themselves when they are young,' said Elizabeth.

'You have very strong opinions for such a young

* At this time, young women of the middle and higher classes were 'out' when they were old enough to go to parties and balls.

person,' said Lady Catherine.

A game of cards followed dinner. Elizabeth found the conversation boring. When Lady Catherine and her daughter had had enough of cards, the carriage was called.

✳✳✳

Sir William returned to Hertfordshire after a week, leaving Elizabeth and Maria at Hunsford. Elizabeth enjoyed half hours of easy conversation with Charlotte, and the weather was fine for long walks. While the others were calling on Lady Catherine, she often walked along the edge of the park. She had found a path between some trees, which no one else seemed to use.

At Easter, two nephews of Lady Catherine arrived at Rosings Park – Mr Darcy was one, the other was a Colonel Fitzwilliam. They called at Hunsford the next day.

Colonel Fitzwilliam was about thirty. He was not handsome, but he was a true gentleman in manners and character. Mr Darcy was unchanged. Colonel Fitzwilliam talked and was charming. Mr Darcy looked out of the window. They did not stay long.

CHAPTER 10
A refusal

As Lady Catherine now had other, more interesting guests, Mr Collins and his party were not needed at Rosings. They did not receive an invitation until the following Sunday, a week after the nephews had arrived.

Lady Catherine was polite, but spoke mostly to Mr Darcy. Colonel Fitzwilliam was very pleased to see Mrs Collins's pretty friend. He now sat next to Elizabeth and talked of travelling and staying at home, of new books and music.

'What are you talking about over there?' called Lady Catherine. She did not like to see a lively conversation and not be at the centre of it.

'We are speaking of music, aunt,' said the Colonel.

And Lady Catherine gave them her views on music for some minutes.

Later Elizabeth was asked to play the piano. Colonel Fitzwilliam sat next to her. During the first song, Mr Darcy came to the piano too.

'Are you trying to frighten me, Mr Darcy, by coming to listen to me? I know I cannot play as well as your sister.

However I become braver when someone tries to frighten me.'

'You know that I do not wish to frighten you, Miss Bennet. But I know that you sometimes enjoy giving opinions that are not your own.'

'Now your cousin will not believe a word I say!' laughed Elizabeth. 'In return I shall have to tell your relations some shocking truths about you that I learned in Hertfordshire.'

'I am not afraid of you,' replied Mr Darcy.

'What did he do wrong?' asked the Colonel. 'I cannot wait to hear.'

'The first time I met him was at a ball in Hertfordshire. At this ball he danced only four dances. And there were not enough gentlemen for all the ladies there.'

'At the time,' answered Mr Darcy, 'I knew only the ladies I came with. And I am not good at meeting strangers.'

'And I am not good at playing the piano. But that is because I do not practise,' said Elizabeth.

✶✶✶

Elizabeth was alone in the house the next morning. She was writing a letter to Jane. There was a ring at the door and a moment later, Mr Darcy came in, alone.

Conversation was difficult. They talked of Rosings and Hunsford. And there were long silences.

Charlotte and her sister then returned from their walk. They were surprised to find Mr Darcy there. After a few minutes, he left.

'What does this mean?' said Charlotte. 'My dear Lizzy, he must be in love with you.'

But Elizabeth told her about the long silences, and

Charlotte's idea seemed less likely. They decided he was bored at Rosings. There was no shooting or fishing at this time of year. Inside there was Lady Catherine.

***

One day Elizabeth met Colonel Fitzwilliam out in the park. She was walking along her favourite path and he joined her. He told her they were leaving Rosings on Saturday, if Darcy did not change his mind again.

'He decides and I follow,' said the Colonel. 'He can do as he likes because he is rich. I, however, am poor.'

'You cannot call yourself poor, Colonel,' said Elizabeth.

'No, but I am not rich enough to marry without thinking of money,' he said.

Elizabeth thought this was meant for her, and quickly changed the subject. She asked if he knew Mr Bingley.

'A little. He is a great friend of Darcy's. Darcy has recently saved him from a bad marriage, I believe. I do not know who the lady was. But Darcy did not think she was good enough for him.'

'And how did Mr Darcy stop his friend?'

'He did not tell me any more than this.'

Back at the house, Elizabeth shut herself in her room. She had thought Caroline Bingley had come between her brother and Jane. Now she learned that it was Darcy! He had destroyed Jane's happiness, because he did not like her family. Elizabeth did not join the others at Rosings for tea that evening – she had a bad headache. Instead she sat by the fire in the sitting room and read again her letters from Jane. She saw her sister's unhappiness in every line.

Suddenly someone knocked at the door. She was amazed when Mr Darcy walked into the room.

He asked if she was better. She answered coldly. He

walked around the room. He sat down. He was silent for some minutes. And then he spoke.

'I cannot control my feelings – they are too strong for me. I must tell you that I love you.'

Elizabeth could not believe it.

He went on. He spoke of his love. But he also spoke of her family. He could not approve of them. Their position in the world was much lower than his. But he hoped she would accept his offer of marriage.

'I *should* thank you for your proposal,' she answered. 'But I cannot. I have never asked for your good opinion. I am sorry to give you pain, and I hope it will not last long.'

Mr Darcy was amazed and angry. 'May I have an explanation for this refusal?'

'Your proposal is clearly designed to offend me. You say you have tried not to like me. But even if I liked you, I could not accept you. You have destroyed my sister's chance of happiness. You have kept Mr Bingley away from her. But even before this, I received a picture of your character from Mr Wickham. You have destroyed his chance of earning a living.'

'So this is your opinion of me!' Mr Darcy cried. 'Is this why you refuse me? Or is it because I was honest about your family and I have hurt your pride? It is not in my character to hide my feelings. You cannot expect me to be happy at the thought of joining my family with yours!'

Elizabeth became angrier with every moment.

'You are wrong, Mr Darcy. I have not refused you because you have offended me. But I am not sorry for refusing you, because you have not acted like a gentleman.'

These words had a strong effect on Mr Darcy, but he said nothing.

'I have seen only pride in you from the very beginning. I felt at once that you were the last man in the world I could ever marry.'

'You have said enough,' he replied. 'Your feelings are clear. Good night.'

Elizabeth sat down and cried for half an hour. When she heard the sound of a carriage outside the house, she hurried upstairs to her room.

CHAPTER 11
The letter

Immediately after breakfast, Elizabeth went out for a walk. The countryside looked beautiful.

Suddenly she saw Mr Darcy walking towards her. He held out a letter.

'Will you please read this?' he asked. He turned away and was gone. Elizabeth opened the letter:

I wish to explain the two offences that have made you angry. You said that I had taken Mr Bingley away from your sister. I had not been in Hertfordshire long when I realised that Bingley liked your sister very much. At the Netherfield ball, however, I learned of the general expectation of a wedding between them. From then on, I watched Bingley closely. I could see that his feelings for your sister were very strong. I watched your sister too. She was open and friendly, but did not seem to be in love. You know her better and perhaps I was wrong. If she is now unhappy because of me, I am sorry. I felt that I must protect my friend when I saw the way that your younger sisters and mother acted at the ball. You and your oldest sister are so very different from the rest of your family.

Bingley left Netherfield for London the next day, but he planned to return. Here is my part. I found that his sisters felt the same as me and we decided to join him in London. I immediately explained to him why I did not approve of the marriage. I did not think that your sister loved him. He does not have a high opinion of himself and he believed me. I do not think I acted badly with the information I had. There is one thing I am not proud of, however. I knew that your sister was in London and I did not tell him. He still does not know.

Now to the second matter. I must tell you the whole history. George Wickham is the son of a very good man, who managed the Pemberley estates. In return for his many years of work, my father was very generous to his son. He paid for Wickham's schooling and had a high opinion of him. He hoped he would become a clergyman. But I had long known the real George. He could not hide his true character from a man of his own age. He was free with women, free with my father's money and paid little attention to his studies.

My father died five years ago and he asked me to find a good church for George, when he was ready. There was one near Pemberley. He also gave him one thousand pounds. Mr Wickham's father died soon after. Six months later, George Wickham wrote to me. He said he did not want to be a clergyman. He planned to study law, and he hoped I would give him money instead of a church. I agreed and gave him three thousand pounds.

I did not expect to see him again. He pretended to study law, but he led a wild life. He lost all the money at cards. Three years later, the church near Pemberley became free. Mr Wickham wrote to me again. He said he had no money and was not enjoying his studies. He would like to be a clergyman and take the church my father had promised. I refused and he was very angry.

This next part gives me great pain. I am sure you will tell no one else. My sister Georgiana is ten years younger than me. A year ago she left school and moved to London. She lived there with a lady called Mrs Younge. Last summer, Mrs Younge took my sister to Ramsgate. Mr Wickham went too. We later learned that Mr Wickham already knew Mrs Younge and that she was a lady of very bad character.

Mr Wickham was very charming to my sister. She believed she was in love with him and agreed to run away with him. She was fifteen. I then arrived in Ramsgate myself. They were not expecting me. As soon as Georgiana saw me, she told me everything. You can imagine how I felt. Mr Wickham was after my sister's fortune, which is thirty thousand pounds. I am sure he also wished to hurt me as much as possible.

This is all true. Please ask Colonel Fitzwilliam if you wish to check - he knows everything.

Yours,

Fitzwilliam Darcy.

Elizabeth began reading this letter with a strong prejudice against everything in it. After reading about Bingley and Jane, she did not feel any differently. But when she read about Wickham, she could not believe it. 'This must be false!' she cried. She read every sentence again and found that it must be true. She went through all her meetings with Wickham in this new light, and everything appeared differently! Wickham gave her very private information the first time they met. He said he was not afraid of Mr Darcy – but he went to London to avoid the Netherfield ball. At first he only told his story to her. He said he was thinking of Mr Darcy's father. But as soon as Darcy was away in London, he happily destroyed his character in front of everyone.

And now she thought of Mr Darcy.

'We have spent a lot of time together in these past weeks. He has done nothing that I do not approve of. His friends and family think very highly of him. He often speaks of his sister with great love. Mr Bingley would not be friends with the man described by Mr Wickham!'

She began to hate herself. 'I was so prejudiced!' she cried. 'I thought I was clever. I thought I could understand good character! Because one man was charming to me, and another was not, I have acted stupidly.'

She now read again the part about Jane. How different it was now! Darcy did not realise Jane's feelings – Charlotte Lucas said the same. And they were right. Jane did not show her feelings. Then she remembered her family at the Netherfield ball – he was right again. She thought of her father. He laughed at her silly sisters, but he did nothing to correct their wildness.

How could she and Jane ever marry well with such a terrible family!

CHAPTER 12
An invitation to Brighton

Elizabeth and Jane arrived back at Longbourn together.

The main news was that the officers were leaving Meryton and going to Brighton for the summer. Lydia and her mother wanted to go too, but Mr Bennet would not allow it.

Elizabeth could not wait to tell Jane all about Darcy, his proposal and the letter about Wickham; she did not tell her, however, anything about Mr Bingley. Jane was amazed at it all.

'Should we tell our friends and family about Mr Wickham's character?' wondered Elizabeth. 'We must say nothing of Mr Darcy's sister, of course. And Mr Wickham is leaving soon. People may find out all about him in the future.' She decided to say nothing about it now.

∗∗∗

As the day approached for the officers to leave, Lydia was sure her heart would break. And then she received an invitation to go to Brighton from the wife of Colonel Forster. Mrs Forster was very young and rather silly. She and Lydia were best friends. Lydia flew around the house, laughing and talking more than ever. Kitty cried, 'Why didn't she ask me? I'm two years older. I should go.' Lydia cared nothing for her sister's feelings. 'You are not her friend,' was all she had to say to Kitty.

Elizabeth went straight to her father.

'She must not go,' said Elizabeth. 'She is too wild already. She will only embarrass her family. If you do not stop her now, it will be too late. Her character will be like this for the rest of her life.' But Elizabeth found she could not move her father.

'No one will think worse of you and Jane because you have three very silly sisters,' he said. 'Colonel Forster is a good man. He will keep her away from trouble. The officers will find better women in Brighton. They will find women who are prettier, have more money and are not so silly. And she will learn her lesson that way. I cannot lock her up for the rest of her life.' Well, Elizabeth had tried. It was easy for Mr Bennet if Lydia went to Brighton and someone else was paying. And he liked an easy life.

And when the officers left Meryton a week later, Lydia packed her bags and went too.

∗∗∗

Life was quiet at Longbourn after that. And then Elizabeth's aunt and uncle, Mr and Mrs Gardiner, invited her to join them on a three-week tour of Derbyshire. The holiday would include a week at Lambton, where Mrs Gardiner had lived before she was married. Elizabeth loved the idea.

Their journey took them through beautiful countryside. When they arrived in Lambton, Elizabeth learned that Pemberley was only five miles away.

'Would you like to visit?' asked Mrs Gardiner as they ate breakfast at their hotel. 'You have heard so much about it. I am sure the housekeeper will show us the house.'

'What would Mr Darcy think if I appeared there?' thought Elizabeth.

'The park is beautiful,' continued Mrs Gardiner. 'They have some of the finest woods in the country.'

Elizabeth discovered from a servant at their hotel that the Darcys were not at Pemberley. In that case, she would love to go!

CHAPTER 13
Pemberley

Elizabeth felt very nervous as the Gardiners' carriage turned into the gates at Pemberley. The park was very large and they drove a long way before they saw the house. They came to the top of a hill and suddenly there it was – a large, handsome, stone building. Behind it were tree-lined hills. In front was a beautiful and natural river. Elizabeth had never seen such a lovely place.

They drove to the front of the house and waited for the housekeeper. Elizabeth began to worry. Perhaps the servant at their hotel was wrong. Perhaps Mr Darcy was really there.

The housekeeper showed them everything with great pride. All the rooms were large, with big windows and fine furniture.

Mr Gardiner asked the housekeeper if Mr Darcy was at home.

'We expect him tomorrow,' said the housekeeper, 'with

a large party of friends.'

'It is lucky we did not come tomorrow!' thought Elizabeth.

Mrs Gardiner found a painting of George Wickham.

'He is now an officer,' explained the housekeeper, 'but I am afraid he is very wild. And over here is Mr Darcy.'

'He has a handsome face,' said Mrs Gardiner. 'Lizzy, is it a good picture of him?'

'Oh!' said the housekeeper. 'Does the young lady know Mr Darcy? Do you not think he is very handsome?'

Elizabeth smiled. 'Yes, very handsome,' she said.

Next was a painting of Miss Darcy.

'Is she as handsome as her brother?' asked Mrs Gardiner.

'Oh yes! She is the most handsome girl you ever saw. And she plays and sings all day long. There is a new piano for her in the next room. Mr Darcy bought it for her. She is coming with him tomorrow.'

'Is Mr Darcy here for much of the year?' asked Mrs Gardiner.

'Only half the year,' replied the housekeeper.

'Perhaps when he marries he will spend more time here,' suggested Mrs Gardiner.

'Yes, but I do not know when that will be. No woman is good enough for him. Everybody here will say the same. He has never spoken a cross word to me in my life, and I have known him since he was four.'

'His father was an excellent man,' said Mrs Gardiner.

'Yes, he was. And his son is just like him – very kind to the poor. Some people call him proud. But I have never seen any pride in him. Perhaps it is because he does not talk all day long like some young men.'

Elizabeth listened closely to the housekeeper's picture.

Everyone here knew Mr Darcy well and they all had a very high opinion of him. She stood in front of a painting and looked at his eyes. She remembered warm looks from him and felt her heart grow.

They thanked the housekeeper and went out into the garden. They walked towards the river and turned back to admire the building. At that moment, from around the side of the house, came Mr Darcy!

Their eyes met. Mr Darcy stopped in surprise. Elizabeth turned away but she could not avoid him. He came towards her and asked polite questions about her family. Neither of them knew what they were saying. He asked the same questions twice more, did not hear the answers and then ran out of ideas. He said goodbye and went into the house.

Elizabeth had never been so embarrassed. Why did she agree to come here? What must he think of her? But he seemed so different. She thought back to their last meeting at Hunsford, when he was so angry. Now he was warm and friendly.

Mr and Mrs Gardiner walked on by the river and Elizabeth followed. They continued through the woods and then came back over a bridge towards the house. Elizabeth was again amazed when Mr Darcy appeared for a second time. He asked her to introduce her friends. Elizabeth prepared for the worst – more Bennet relatives! He did not hurry away, however, but began a conversation about fishing with Mr Gardiner. Elizabeth listened carefully and enjoyed her uncle's good manners and intelligence as he spoke. Mr Darcy then invited Mr Gardiner to spend a day fishing at Pemberley.

'Why is he so changed?' thought Elizabeth. 'It cannot be for me. It is impossible that he still loves me.'

The four of them walked on. The Gardiners were slower and fell behind. Mr Darcy walked with Elizabeth.

'Your housekeeper was sure you were coming tomorrow,' she said. 'Or we would not be here.'

'I am a day early,' he said. 'Mr Bingley and his sisters come tomorrow. My sister is also coming. I would very much like to introduce her to you.'

Elizabeth said she would be very pleased to meet her. She knew now that he still had feelings for her.

✳✳✳

The next morning, Mr Darcy arrived at the hotel in Lambton with his sister. Elizabeth had heard that Miss Darcy was very proud. In fact, she was extremely shy. She was tall and less handsome than her brother, but with a lovely character. Mr Bingley came too and he was very pleased to see her. Although he asked about all Elizabeth's sisters, his questions were clearly about Jane. As they were leaving, Mr Darcy invited the Gardiners and Elizabeth to dinner at Pemberley the next evening. They accepted at once. It was quite clear to the Gardiners that Mr Darcy was in love with Elizabeth. They were not sure what her opinion of him was. They did not want to embarrass Elizabeth, however, and they did not ask.

That night Elizabeth lay awake. She tried to understand her feelings. She certainly did not hate Mr Darcy. She was sorry for her first opinion of him. And she was moved by his love for her.

CHAPTER 14
Terrible news

Mrs Gardiner and Elizabeth returned Miss Darcy's visit the next morning. The gentlemen were out, and they took tea with Miss Darcy and Louisa and Caroline Bingley. Miss Darcy was almost too shy to speak. The Bingley sisters welcomed them coldly.

The servants brought tea and cakes, and Mr Darcy appeared. Miss Bingley watched him closely and it was clear she still hoped to win him. She wanted to embarrass Elizabeth and asked about the officers at Meryton. She did not know about Wickham and Miss Darcy. She did not know what pain she gave to Miss Darcy and her brother. Elizabeth cleverly moved the subject away from Wickham, and Mr Darcy gave her a grateful look. Elizabeth and her aunt left soon after this conversation.

'Elizabeth Bennet has changed since we last saw her, Mr Darcy,' said Caroline Bingley after they had gone. 'She is so brown! Her face is too thin and she is not pretty. I know her eyes are sometimes called "fine", but I think they are ordinary. I remember, when we first saw her in Hertfordshire, you thought she was rather pretty!'

'Yes,' said Mr Darcy. 'But that was only when I first knew her. I now think she is one of the most beautiful women I have ever met.'

***

The next morning Elizabeth and her uncle and aunt were preparing to go for a walk. The post arrived, bringing two letters from Jane.

'Would I offend you if I stayed to read my letters?' Elizabeth asked.

'Of course not,' said her aunt. 'Your uncle and I will take a walk to the church and call back for you in an hour.'

Jane's first letter had the wrong address, and had taken an extra day to reach Lambton.

Elizabeth opened that one first.

My dearest Lizzy, we are all well, but I have some bad news. An urgent letter came to Longbourn at twelve last night. We had just gone to bed. It was from Colonel Forster. Poor Lydia, he told us, has run off with one of his officers – with Wickham!

I am very, very sorry. It is such a silly marriage for both of them. Our poor mother is very unhappy. Colonel Forster is on his way to Longbourn. I will write again as soon as we have more news.

Elizabeth pulled open the second letter. It was written a day later.

My dearest sister, I hardly know what to write. The news is worse. Colonel Forster learnt from Mr Denny in Brighton that Mr Wickham and poor Lydia are not married. Colonel Forster spoke to Mr Denny in Brighton. Mr Denny told him that Wickham never meant to marry Lydia. Colonel Forster tried to follow Wickham and Lydia's path, but they changed carriages halfway to London. He asked at all the stopping places on the way to London, but no one had heard of them. Then he came to Longbourn. Our father and mother fear the worst. But I cannot believe it. Impossible! Lydia is not so silly. I am sure they have married in private for some reason. Poor mother is really ill and will not leave her bed. I never saw our father so upset. He is leaving for London now. Colonel Forster has had to return to Brighton. I am sure Father would be very grateful for our uncle's help. Lizzy, please come home.

'Oh! Where is my uncle?' cried Elizabeth when she had read the letters. She ran to the door. At that moment, a servant opened it and in walked Mr Darcy.

'What is the matter?' he asked, when he saw her pale face. 'Are you ill?'

'Please find my uncle. I have had the most terrible news from Longbourn!' Elizabeth began to cry.

Mr Darcy sent the servant to find Mr Gardiner. He helped Elizabeth to a seat.

'My sister Lydia has left all her friends and has run away with … Mr Wickham. They have gone off together from Brighton. She is lost! Why did I not say anything about his character?'

'I am shocked,' said Darcy. 'Who is looking for them?'

'My father has gone to London. Jane has asked for my uncle's help. We will return immediately. But nothing can be done. It is hopeless.'

Darcy was walking up and down the room. He was deep in thought and his face was serious. Elizabeth knew that he could never be part of her family now. And she felt, for the first time, that she loved him.

And then he spoke. 'I am sure you want me to go. There is nothing I can do or say … I am afraid my sister will not be able to see you at Pemberley today.'

'Oh yes. Please say sorry to your sister for us. Tell her that we have important business at home suddenly. Please hide the truth for as long as possible … I know it cannot be long.'

Mr Darcy left.

'I will never see him again,' thought Elizabeth.

CHAPTER 15
Back at Longbourn

The next day Elizabeth and the Gardiners arrived back at Longbourn. Mr Gardiner left at once for London. Mrs Gardiner followed a few days later. Jane and Elizabeth waited at home for news. Jane had no extra information to give her sister, except that Wickham had to leave Brighton quickly because he had lost a thousand pounds at cards.

The arrival of the post was now the most important part of the day at Longbourn. News came from London that there was no news.

Mr Bennet and Mr Gardiner were looking all over London for Lydia and Wickham. A letter came from Mr Collins, which Jane opened. He said he was very sorry to hear of the terrible business:

> *The death of Lydia would be better than this. My dear wife tells me that Lydia has always been wild. But I think her character must be naturally bad if she acts this way when she is so young. Lady Catherine says that this false step in one daughter will hurt the fortunes of all the others. As she says, who would join themselves to such a family?*

Mr Bennet returned home. He had failed to find them. He did not want to talk much, but to Elizabeth he said, 'I am sorry I did not listen to you last May. You told me not to let Lydia go to Brighton, and you were right.'

Two days later, a letter came from Mr Gardiner. Jane and Elizabeth ran with the letter to their father, who was walking in the garden.

Mr Bennet read:

I have seen them both, they are not married. If you agree to the following terms, however, Wickham will marry Lydia. Lydia will have her thousand pounds after you and my sister die. During your life, you will pay her one hundred pounds a year. Please send your answer. There is no time to lose.

'Is it possible?' cried Elizabeth. 'Is it possible that he will marry her?'

'Oh, this is good news,' said Jane.

'No sensible man would marry Lydia for so little money,' said Mr Bennet to Jane and Elizabeth. 'How much has your uncle paid out for this? How will I ever pay it back?'

Mr Bennet felt he was a lucky man. He knew it was all his fault. He had not paid enough attention to his daughters. He was very ashamed of himself. However, he felt these feelings would quickly pass. The whole thing was costing him very little and he would soon be able to return to his books in the library.

The effect of the news on Mrs Bennet was immediate. She got up from her bed. She prepared to visit her sister in Meryton and call on Lady Lucas on the way home. 'My dear, dear Lydia!' she cried. 'She will be married at sixteen. I can't wait to see her. And dear Wickham too! But we must think about the wedding clothes! I am so happy. Mrs Wickham! It sounds lovely.'

✳✳✳

Elizabeth's thoughts returned to Pemberley. She now believed that Mr Darcy was the perfect man for her. Her lively character and easy manners would help his shyness. And she could learn so much from his understanding of the world. But no such happy marriage could now take place. Mr Darcy would never marry into a family that included Wickham.

More news came from Mr Gardiner. After the wedding, Mr and Mrs Wickham would move to the north of the country and Mr Wickham would stay an officer. All his bills were now paid. And Mr and Mrs Wickham wished to visit Longbourn before their journey to Newcastle.

CHAPTER 16
The truth

A carriage drove up to the door and Mr and Mrs Wickham got out. Nothing in the last fortnight had changed Lydia. She was as wild as ever, and very pleased with herself. She talked and did not listen. Wickham was as charming as always. They were ashamed of nothing.

Elizabeth kept away from Lydia and Wickham when she could. But one morning, Lydia came and sat next to her sister.

'Lizzy, I never told you about my wedding. You were not there when I told the others. Do you not want to hear about it?'

'No,' replied Elizabeth. 'We should say as little as possible about it.'

'You are so strange, Lizzy! Well, listen, now. We went to the church from Aunt Gardiner's at eleven o'clock. And there was my aunt – she talked to me all the time like a clergyman, like Mr Collins! I did not listen, because I was thinking about my dear Wickham. Would he wear a blue coat or a red one? Anyway, we got to the church at the same time as Mr Darcy …'

'Mr Darcy!' repeated Elizabeth.

'Oh yes! He came with Wickham, you know. But – oh dear! – I forgot – it was a secret.'

∗∗∗

Elizabeth ran to her room and wrote at once to her aunt for an explanation. A reply came by the next post. Her aunt was very surprised that Elizabeth did not already know about Mr Darcy's part in the business.

Mr Darcy left Derbyshire the day after us and went to London. He found Mr Wickham and your sister. He made Mr Wickham an offer and then came to see Mr Gardiner. He arranged everything himself and would accept no help. Your uncle wanted to pay for Lydia, but Mr Darcy would not allow it. Not only that, but he said the world must think your uncle had paid! Your uncle does not like this arrangement at all, as you can imagine. You, at least, will know the truth. The cost of all this to Mr Darcy is around three thousand pounds, I believe. He says it was his fault that the world did not know about Mr Wickham's character. He kept it secret because of his pride. I like him very much, Lizzy. He has been so kind to us.

Elizabeth's heart whispered that he had done this for her. Her head told her that he had not – he had given her aunt a good reason for his actions. But he had saved her family's good name. She was proud of him. He had done this because it was the right thing to do. He had not thought of his own feelings.

CHAPTER 17
Another proposal

Lydia and Mr Wickham left for Newcastle and the house was quiet again. Only Mrs Bennet missed her youngest daughter's laugh. In fact, she was quite fed up until her sister Mrs Philips brought her some happy news. The housekeeper at Netherfield was opening up the house and Mr Bingley was arriving in a day or two. He was coming for the shooting season.

When Jane heard the news, she changed colour. She and Lizzy had not talked of Bingley for many weeks.

'I am not upset,' she said to Lizzy later, when they were alone. 'I have no feelings for him now. But I hate to hear our mother talk about it all the time.'

Elizabeth did not know what to think. Did he still love Jane? Did Mr Darcy now approve of his friend's feelings? She did not know what to say to her sister

The news came that Mr Bingley had arrived. Mrs Bennet planned to wait three days and then send him an invitation to dinner.

But on the third morning after his arrival, Kitty suddenly called:

'Mama. Mr Bingley is coming. Look!'

Jane did not move. Elizabeth felt her shock.

'And there is someone with him,' Kitty went on. 'It's that tall, proud man – what was his name?'

'Mr Darcy!' said Mrs Bennet. 'Well, any friend of Mr Bingley's is always welcome here. But I do not like him at all.'

Elizabeth was amazed. Why had Mr Darcy come to Netherfield, to Longbourn? Did he still love her? She did not know.

The visit was uncomfortable. Bingley looked both pleased and embarrassed. Jane did not say much. Mr Darcy said almost nothing and watched Jane or looked at the ground. Mrs Bennet spoke more than enough for everyone. She was too polite to Mr Bingley and very rude to Mr Darcy. Both daughters were ashamed of her. Elizabeth was more ashamed because she knew what Mr Darcy had done for Mrs Bennet. He had saved her favourite daughter. Mrs Bennet talked about Lydia.

'They have gone to Newcastle, in the north, where Mr Wickham has found a new position,' she said, looking at Mr Darcy. 'Thank goodness he has *some* friends!'

Elizabeth had never been so embarrassed in her life. She could not look at Mr Darcy.

The two men were invited to dinner at Longbourn on the following Tuesday and they left soon after.

✳✳✳

Elizabeth and Jane went into the garden.

'Now the first meeting is over,' said Jane. 'I feel easier.

I will not be embarrassed again. When he comes on Tuesday, everyone will see that we are just friends.'

'Everyone will see,' smiled her sister, 'that he loves you just as much as before!'

∗∗∗

On Tuesday there was a large party at Longbourn. Mr Bingley sat next to Jane at dinner. During the evening, his admiration for her became more and more clear.

Mr Darcy sat a long way from Elizabeth, near her mother. She could not hear their conversation, but she could see how cold they were to each other. After dinner, she hoped he would talk to her. Other guests were in the way, however, and there was no chance of it. After the guests had left, everyone was pleased with the evening except Elizabeth.

'I refused him!' she told herself. 'What man would make a second proposal to the same woman?'

∗∗∗

A few days later, Mr Bingley came to Longbourn alone. Mr Darcy had gone to London, he explained, but would return in a few days' time. Mr Bingley was invited to stay for supper and invited again the next morning to shoot birds with Mr Bennet. Nobody questioned his feelings now, not even Jane.

Mr Bingley and Mr Bennet spent a fine morning together and they returned for lunch. Elizabeth went into the breakfast room after tea to write a letter. The others played cards. Elizabeth returned to the sitting room and found Bingley and her sister alone. They stood together by the fire but Bingley quickly moved away when she came in. Bingley whispered to Jane and ran out of the room.

'I am so happy, Lizzy,' said Jane, and ran into her sister's arms. 'I wish everybody was as happy as me.'

Elizabeth was happier for her sister than she could ever say in words.

'I must tell Mother,' said Jane. 'Mr Bingley has gone to ask Father.'

CHAPTER 18
An unexpected visitor

About a week after this happy engagement, a carriage drove up to the house. Elizabeth, Kitty and their mother were in the sitting room. The door opened and in came Lady Catherine de Bourgh.

She sat down without a word. Mrs Bennet had never had such an important visitor and, for once, was not able to speak.

'That lady, I imagine, is your mother,' said Lady Catherine to Elizabeth. 'And this must be one of your sisters.'

'Yes, Lady Catherine,' said Elizabeth.

'You have a very small park here,' she said, after a short silence. 'Miss Bennet, I saw a pretty walk in the garden. Would you come for a walk there with me? I wish to speak to you.' They went outside.

'I am sure you know the reason for my visit,' began Lady Catherine.

'I have no idea, Lady Catherine,' Elizabeth replied.

'Miss Bennet, do not play games with me. Two days ago I heard some shocking news. Not only is your sister about to make a *very* good marriage. But you are likely to marry my nephew, Mr Darcy, soon after! I know this cannot be true. It is impossible. What do you have to say?'

'If you know this cannot be true, why are you asking me?' said Elizabeth.

'Answer me! Has my nephew asked you to marry him?'

'You said it was impossible.'

'It ought to be impossible. But perhaps you have practised your female arts on him! I am almost his nearest relative and I have a right to know his business.'

'But you have no right to know mine.'

'Mr Darcy is engaged to my daughter!'

'Then he will not make a proposal to me,' replied Elizabeth.

'It is an unusual engagement. It was decided between me and his mother when our children were born. Will you go against the wishes of his family?'

'I can only accept him if I am his choice.'

'If you marry Mr Darcy, the family will never speak your name again.'

'That would certainly be awful.'

'I am ashamed of you. What about your family?'

'Mr Darcy is a gentleman. I am a gentleman's daughter. If your nephew accepts my family, why should not you?'

'Tell me, Miss Bennet! Are you engaged to my nephew?'

'I am not!'

Lady Catherine looked pleased.

'And will you promise never to be engaged to him?'

'I will not.'

'Miss Bennet, I am shocked. I shall not leave until I have a promise.'

'I shall never give one.'

'I have one more thing to say. I know all about your younger sister and Mr Wickham. Can this girl be my nephew's sister? Can her husband be his brother? What are you thinking of? Is Pemberley to be brought so low?'

'Lady Catherine, you have offended me in every way possible. I am returning to the house.' Elizabeth walked quickly back through the garden.

'I am seriously displeased, you ungrateful girl,' shouted Lady Catherine after her.

Elizabeth heard the carriage drive away.

'Was she bringing news from Hunsford of Mr and Mrs Collins?' asked her mother.

'Yes,' replied Elizabeth, not quite telling the truth.

CHAPTER 19
A walk

Within a few days of Lady Catherine's visit, Mr Bingley arrived with Mr Darcy. They suggested a walk. Bingley and Jane walked off quickly, and soon Mr Darcy and Elizabeth were walking alone.

'Mr Darcy, I am so grateful for your kindness to my poor sister.'

Darcy was surprised.

'It was not my aunt's fault,' Elizabeth said quickly. 'Lydia told me your secret. Then I had to find out the rest. So let me thank you, for my family.'

'If you must thank me,' he said, 'please thank me for yourself alone. I thought only of you.'

They walked on in silence. Then Mr Darcy spoke again.

'If your feelings are the same as they were last April, tell me so at once. My feelings are unchanged; but one word from you will be the end of it.'

Elizabeth told him that her feelings were now quite the opposite. He had never been so happy. He told her how much he loved her.

They walked on, but they had no idea where. There was so much to talk about. Darcy told Elizabeth that his aunt had come to London from Longbourn and repeated her conversation with Elizabeth to him.

'That gave me hope,' he said. 'You did not tell her that an engagement was impossible. And I know that you always speak the truth.'

Elizabeth said she was very sorry that she refused his first proposal so rudely.

'Your facts were wrong, but you were right,' said Darcy. 'I did not speak to you like a gentleman. Did my letter make you think better of me?'

She explained that it had removed all her prejudices against him.

'And you, dearest Elizabeth, have taught me a lesson. You have shown me my pride.'

CHAPTER 20
Two weddings

That night, Elizabeth opened her heart to Jane.

'You are joking, Lizzy. This cannot be! Engaged to Mr Darcy! No, no. It is impossible.'

'If you do not believe me,' laughed Elizabeth, 'nobody else will!'

The next evening, Mr Darcy spoke to Mr Bennet. Then her father sent Mr Darcy out and called Elizabeth in.

'Are you sure, Lizzy?' he asked. 'Have you not always hated this man? Is he not the proudest man we have ever met?'

'I love him,' she said, with tears in her eyes. 'He is not proud.'

She described Mr Darcy's character to her father. She told him what he had done for Lydia. Her father was amazed and pleased. He would offer to pay the money back to Mr Darcy, and Mr Darcy would refuse. Nothing could be better!

'If any young men come for Kitty or Mary,' he said to Elizabeth as she left the room, 'send them in!'

Then Elizabeth told her mother. For at least ten minutes, Mrs Bennet was unable to say a word. And then the words came.

'Dear me! Mr Darcy! Lizzy! How rich and great you will be! Oh my sweetest Lizzy. What carriages you will have! I am so pleased – so happy! Such a charming man! So tall! So handsome! I am sorry I didn't like him before. Dear, dear Lizzy! A house in London! Three daughters married. Ten thousand a year! My dear, what is Mr Darcy's favourite dish? We shall have it tomorrow.'

***

Mr Bingley and Jane stayed a year at Netherfield. It was perhaps a little too near to Jane's mother and Meryton relatives, even for them. They bought an estate only thirty miles from Pemberley.

Kitty spent most of her time with her two older sisters and became a very fine young woman. Although Mrs Wickham invited Kitty often to stay, her father would never allow it. Lydia often wrote to Elizabeth too, generally to ask for money.

Mr Darcy's sister came back to live at Pemberley, and Elizabeth and she became close friends.

Caroline Bingley was not at all pleased with Mr Darcy's marriage. She wished to continue to visit Pemberley, however, and tried to be polite to Elizabeth. Even Lady Catherine came to visit in the end. She wanted to see how Mr Darcy's wife managed things at Pemberley and, of course, to give her some advice.

The Darcys were the best of friends with the Gardiners. Darcy loved them as much as Elizabeth. They had brought Elizabeth to Derbyshire, and for that, Elizabeth and Darcy would always be very grateful.

THE END

Jane Austen:

Then

Jane Austen was born in 1775 in a village in Hampshire, in the south of England. She was the daughter of a clergyman and had six brothers and a sister, Cassandra.

Jane came from an intelligent family. The Austens loved books and reading. The family also liked acting and Jane often wrote plays for them. She started writing her first book when she was just 14.

When Jane was 20, she fell in love with a young Irishman called Tom Lefroy. She said that his only fault was that 'his morning coat was too light'. However, Lefroy was not a rich man and so marriage was not possible. Soon after meeting Lefroy, Jane started work on *Pride and Prejudice*.

In 1802, the family moved to the town of Bath. While in Bath, a rich man, Harris Bigg-Wither, proposed to Jane.

At first she accepted his proposal but overnight, she changed her mind.

When Jane's father died, Jane, her mother and her sister moved to Hampshire near their brother, Edward. Jane did most of her writing there.

Jane's first book, *Sense and Sensibility* was published in 1811. This was followed by *Pride and Prejudice* in 1813, *Mansfield Park* in 1814 and *Emma* in 1815. All were published anonymously. This was usual for women writers at that time, although some women writers used men's names.

In 1817, at the age of 41, Jane died after a long illness. Her last two books, *Persuasion* and *Northanger Abbey*, were published after her death. Her name appeared on the covers for the first time.

then and now

Now

Today, almost 200 years later, Jane Austen's books are more popular than ever. But why are stories about life in 18th century England still so interesting to us? Jane Austen watched people closely and wrote about them in a lively and funny way. We can see the characters in her books in our world today. *Pride and Prejudice* is Jane Austen's best-known book. It has inspired many film-makers and writers. *Bridget Jones's Diary* by Helen Fielding (2001) is set in modern day London, but follows the main story of *Pride and Prejudice*. When Bridget first meets Mark Darcy, a handsome young lawyer, she doesn't like him at all.

However, by the end of the story, Bridget feels very differently …

In 2005, Keira Knightley, star of *Pirates of the Caribbean*, played Lizzy Bennet in a new film of *Pride and Prejudice* and recently it was voted Britain's second best-loved book. Jane Austen and her stories of love and marriage in small English towns are here here to stay!

Discuss. Which classics writers are most famous in your country? Why are they still popular, do you think?

'Helen Fielding is one of the funniest writers in Britain and Bridget Jones is a creation of comic genius'
NICK HORNBY

BRIDGETJONES'S**DIARY**
HELEN FIELDING

Jane AUSTEN
Pride and Prejudice
A Classic Romance

HEALTH WARNING

What do these words mean? You can use a dictionary.
publish   anonymous   character   inspire   lawyer   classics

"A young man with a large fortune is coming to live at Netherfield Park! His name is Bingley and he is single! What a fine thing for our girls!"

Love &

Pride and Prejudice is a book about marriage. Mrs Bennet's main goal in life is to have five married daughters. But why was marriage so important to women at that time?

Money

In Jane Austen's time, money was extremely important. Young ladies, like the Bennet sisters, did not work or have their own money. They had to stay with their families until they got married. This put a lot of pressure on women to accept proposals of marriage, especially from rich men.

Elizabeth's friend, Charlotte Lucas, is neither pretty nor rich. At 27 years old, she is also getting too old to be single. She accepts Mr Collins's proposal, because she wants a home and a husband. Her own romantic feelings have nothing to do with her choice.

The Bennet family and their friends are not rich, like Mr Darcy and the Bingleys. Mr Bennet's estate will go to Mr Collins when he dies, as there are no sons. With no real money or property, the Bennet sisters have to depend on their good looks and natural charm to find a husband – and a place to live.

Being respectable

In Regency England, respectable unmarried women did not spend time alone with

men. When Lydia runs away with Wickham, it is one of the worst things to happen to the Bennet family. Usually this would mean that no respectable gentlemen would want to marry any of the other sisters. Luckily, Mr Darcy's money and love for Elizabeth save the family's good name.

Marriage
n Regency* England

* The Regency period is the time between 1811 and 1820. King George III's son, the Prince Regent, ruled at that time.

Make a list of the characters in *Pride and Prejudice* who are married. What kind of marriages do they have, do you think? Are they happy?

Finding a husband

How did young men and women meet and become engaged in Jane Austen's time? Dances were very important. Men could show interest in a woman by dancing with her several times at a ball.

Men and women could also visit each other. The girl's mother, or a married female relative, would always be at any meeting. Young women could also nvite each other to their homes. In this way, Jane spends time with Bingley at Netherfield at the start of *Pride and Prejudice*.

Even when a couple were engaged, they couldn't spend lots of time alone together. Engagements were short. Often when people got married, they didn't really know their husband or wife at all. Lots of marriages in the 18th and 19th centuries were very unhappy for this reason.

What do these words mean?
You can use a dictionary.
pressure especially property charm
respectable period

Socialising in Regency* England

Socialising was very important in Jane Austen's day. For young women, it was the only way of meeting new men – and finding a husband!

* The Regency period is the time between 1811 and 1820. King George III's son, the Prince Regent, ruled at that time.

Being 'out'

'Are any of your younger sisters out?' Lady Catherine asked.

'Yes, all of them,' replied Elizabeth.

'All five out at once! How strange!'

Being 'out' meant being allowed to go to balls, dinners and other social events. Young ladies always went with their mothers, or an older married relative or friend. Often younger unmarried daughters only came 'out' once their older sisters were married. Lady Catherine is surprised that the younger sisters are already 'out' when Jane and Elizabeth are still unmarried. She does not think this is a good thing!

Time out

Dancing was very popular in Regency England. During a dance, unmarried men and women could talk, and even touch each other – as part of the dance!

Jane Austen loved dancing. There were lots of places to go. Rich people, like the Bingleys, might have big private balls. There were also public dances called 'assemblies'.

There were usually about ten dances in an evening. The men always asked the ladies to dance – a woman couldn't ask a man. It was also seen as impolite to refuse a partner.

Dances usually lasted until the early morning. There was always food of some kind – at a ball, there was usually a dinner in the middle of the evening. At a dance, there was often a room where people could sit and play cards. Many people played for money. Card playing was popular with men and women.

Time in

Rich women and men in Jane Austen's world had a lot of free time. They didn't have jobs. During the day, young ladies might spend time doing embroidery, sewing or reading. Some homes had a piano, and women learnt to play and sing. In the afternoons, families might visit their friends and neighbours.

Many evenings were spent at home with family and friends. Often a group of people sat in the same room doing different things. One person might read, others might play cards and someone else might play the piano. Sometimes, people walked around the room, making conversation! In *Pride and Prejudice*, Caroline asks Elizabeth to join her for a walk, because she wants Mr Darcy to notice her.

1 Compare social life in Regency England with your social life today. What is the same? What is different?

2 Why was being 'out' so important for young girls like Lydia and Kitty?

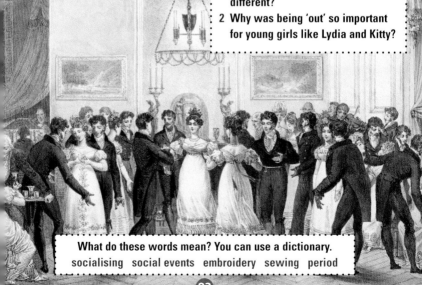

What do these words mean? You can use a dictionary.
socialising   social events   embroidery   sewing   period

CHAPTERS 1 – 3

Before you read
Use a dictionary for this section.

1 Look at the New Words at the back of the book.
  a) Which of these people works in a church?
    a servant   a nephew   a clergyman
  b) Which of these is somewhere that a rich person lives?
    an estate   a fortune   a carriage
  c) Which of these means to upset somebody?
    admire   embarrass   offend
  d) Which word describes someone who is nice, friendly and polite?
    charming   shocking   ashamed
  e) Which of these mean you are going to marry?
    embarrassed   engaged   shocked

2 Look at People and places on pages 4–5.
  a) Who does Mr Darcy not like?
  b) Who is the youngest of the five Bennet girls?
  c) Who is very rich and has a rich nephew?
  d) Who comes to live near the Bennets?
  e) Who is a relative of the Bennets?

After you read
3 Answer these questions.
  a) Why does Mrs Bennet hope Mr Bingley will marry one of her daughters before she even meets him?
  b) Mr Darcy pays no attention to the Bennet girls at the Meryton ball. What does Mrs Bennet think of him?
  c) Mr Bingley admires Jane. Does he know how Jane feels?
  d) Mr Darcy begins to admire Elizabeth at the Lucases. Does Elizabeth know?
  e) Caroline Bingley is moving to Netherfield with her brother. What does she think of her country neighbours?
  f) Jane is ill. Why is Mrs Bennet pleased?

g) Caroline Bingley is interested in Mr Darcy. Does he feel the same about her?

h) Is Elizabeth frightened by her rich neighbours at Netherfield Park?

4 What do you think?
Charlotte Lucas says, 'Happiness in marriage happens by chance.' Is this true today?

5 Writing
Elizabeth keeps a diary while she is staying at Netherfield. Write her diary.

Example: *Thursday: I had a lovely walk to Netherfield this morning. Jane is really ill.*

CHAPTERS 4 – 7

Before you read

6 One day, when Mr Bennet dies, Longbourn will belong to Mr Collins. Why do you think he is coming to visit the Bennets?

After you read

7 Are these sentences right or wrong?

a) Lady Catherine is the most important thing in Mr Collins's world.

b) Elizabeth is Mr Collins's first choice for a wife.

c) Mr Darcy and Mr Wickham have met before.

d) Mr Wickham has a good reason to not like Mr Darcy.

e) At the Netherfield ball, Mr Darcy and Elizabeth enjoy their dance together.

f) Elizabeth is ashamed of everyone in her family at the ball except Jane.

g) Mr Bennet wants Elizabeth to accept Mr Collins's proposal.

h) Elizabeth does not approve of Charlotte Lucas's decision to marry Mr Collins.

8 What do you think?
- **a)** Jane thinks Caroline Bingley is kind and a good friend. Elizabeth thinks she says one thing and thinks another. Who do you think is right?
- **b)** Is Elizabeth right to refuse Mr Collins? Why/Why not?

9 Writing
Mrs Bennet hears about the marriage between Mr Collins and Charlotte Lucas. She has several reasons to be angry. She writes to her sister Mrs Gardiner in London. Write her letter and say why you are angry.

CHAPTERS 8 – 11

Before you read

10 Think about these questions.
- **a)** The Bingleys and Mr Darcy are in London. Jane goes to London to stay with her uncle and aunt. Will she see Mr Bingley there, do you think?
- **b)** There is a proposal and a refusal in this section. Who will ask someone to marry them? Who will say 'No'?

After you read

11 Complete these sentences.
- **a)** Jane decides that Elizabeth was right about …
- **b)** Mr Wickham decides that Miss King (with ten thousand a year) is more attractive than …
- **c)** … has strong opinions about everything.
- **d)** Elizabeth learns from Colonel Fitzwilliam that … has kept Bingley away from Jane.
- **e)** Mr Darcy proposes to Elizabeth although he does not like …

12 What do you think?
Elizabeth changes her mind about Mr Darcy completely after reading his letter. Are you surprised by his letter? Do you believe him?

13 Writing
Imagine Elizabeth meets Mr Wickham just after she reads Mr Darcy's letter. Write their conversation.

CHAPTERS 12 – 15

Before you read

14 Write your ideas.

    a) Chapter 12 is called *An invitation to Brighton*. Who will go to Brighton, do you think?

    b) Chapter 13 is called *Pemberley*. Who will meet at Pemberley?

    c) Chapter 14 is called *Terrible news*. What will the terrible news be?

    d) Chapter 15 is called *Back at Longbourn*. Who do you think is back there?

After you read

15 Which of these actions are mistakes?

    a) Elizabeth decides not to tell her friends and family about Mr Wickham's real character.

    b) Mr Bennet allows Lydia to go to Brighton.

    c) Elizabeth agrees to visit Pemberley.

    d) Elizabeth allows her feelings for Mr Darcy to grow.

    e) Mr Gardiner arranges Wickham and Lydia's wedding.

16 What do you think?
Will Lydia and Mr Wickham have a happy marriage? Why / why not?

17 Work in threes. Imagine Mr and Mrs Collins go to Rosings Park with the news from Longbourn.
Student A: You are Mr Collins. Tell Lady Catherine that Lydia has run off with Mr Wickham.
Student B: You are Mrs Collins. Tell Lady Catherine that Lydia has always been wild.
Student C: You are Lady Catherine. Express your opinions strongly.

18 Writing
When Mrs Bennet hears about Lydia and Wickham's wedding, she sends a note to all her friends. She gives them the news. Write her note.

CHAPTERS 16 – 20

Before you read

19 Mr Gardiner has saved the Bennet family name. How will these people feel?
  a) Jane and Elizabeth
  b) Mr Darcy
   c) Lady Catherine de Bourgh
  d) Mr Collins
  e) Lady Lucas

20 Write your ideas.
  a) Mr Darcy will marry
     Caroline Bingley   **Miss de Bourgh**   **Elizabeth**
  b) Mr Bingley will marry
     Georgiana Darcy   **Miss de Bourgh**   **Jane**

After you read

21 Who says these things? Who are they speaking to?
  a) 'I hope we can still be friends now we are brother and sister.'
  b) 'Please come to dinner on Tuesday. And you may bring your friend if you wish.'
  c) 'Will you marry me and come and live at Netherfield Park?'
  d) 'You will not believe how rude that girl was. I am so glad you are not thinking of marrying her!'
  e) 'I always liked him! Even when other people said he was proud!'

22 What do you think?
  a) Is it a good ending?
  b) Do you prefer happy endings or shocking endings?

23 Writing
  a) How many different reasons for getting married are there in this story? Write a list.
  b) Imagine you are one of these characters. Describe how you feel at the end of the story.
     Caroline Bingley   **Mr Bennet**   **Mrs Bennet**
     Mr Collins   **Mr Wickham**